Princess Poppy
The Fashion Princess

Check out Princess Poppy's website
to find out all about the other
books in the series

www.princesspoppy.com

Princess Poppy
The Fashion
Princess

written by Janey Louise Jones
Illustrated by Samantha Chaffey

THE FASHION PRINCESS
A YOUNG CORGI BOOK 978 0 552 55953 9

Published in Great Britain by Young Corgi,
an imprint of Random House Children's Publishers UK
A Random House Group Company

First published in 2008
This edition published in 2011

The Random House Group Limited supports The Forest Stewardship Council
(FSC®), the leading international forest certification organisation. Our books
carrying the FSC label are printed on FSC® certified paper. FSC is the only forest
certification scheme endorsed by the leading environmental organisations,
including Greenpeace. Our paper procurement policy can be found at
www.randomhouse.co.uk/environment

MIX
Paper from
responsible sources
FSC   FSC® C016897
www.fsc.org

Set in 15/21pt Bembo MT Schoolbook by
Falcon Oast Graphic Art Ltd.

Young Corgi Books are published by Random House Children's Publishers UK,
61–63 Uxbridge Road, London W5 5SA

www.**princesspoppy**.com
www.**randomhousechildrens**.co.uk

Addresses for companies within The Random House Group Limited
can be found at: www.randomhouse.co.uk/offices.htm

THE RANDOM HOUSE GROUP Limited Reg. No. 954009

A CIP catalogue record for this book is available from the British Library.

Printed and bound by CPI Group (UK) Ltd, Croydon, CR0 4YY

*For the real Berry Coleman
and all independent thinkers*

Chapter One

Poppy looked through the aircraft
window, desperate for her first peek of
New York City. She could hardly believe
what she saw, even though she had seen
pictures in her guide book, the real thing
was even more amazing. The needle-point
skyscrapers looked like space rockets
about to lift off, and there were masses of
neon lights and thousands and thousands
of cars driving through the busy streets in
the early evening light. Everything looked

twinkly. The view was completely alien to Poppy. She was used to the gentle rolling countryside around Honeypot Hill, where little cottages nestled cosily in the dales and the roads were almost empty of cars. She couldn't wait to explore the city!

Just then the captain announced that they should strap themselves in because the plane would be landing in ten minutes. As the plane descended, Poppy looked from her guide book to the window, trying to see whether she could spot some of the sights she had read about. What she really wanted to see was the Statue of Liberty. It looked so beautiful and she was fascinated by its history. Saffron had explained to her during the flight that the statue had been given to the Americans by the French in 1886 as a sign of friendship and to celebrate American independence.

As they waited to get off the plane, Poppy admired the outfits of all the beautiful and glamorous people filing past them along the aisle.

"Oh, look, Poppy. That's Tallulah Melage, the famous supermodel," whispered a star-struck Saffron, pointing to a tall, willowy girl with dark-blonde hair.

Tallulah was wearing a white raincoat tightly belted round her waist, with a hot pink scarf at her swan-like neck. Her long hair was tied in a loose ponytail and she had dark glasses propped up on her head.

Poppy gasped. "A *real* model! Wow! She's really, really beautiful."

"I know," agreed Saffron, "and she's so *incredibly* stylish too. I can't believe we've seen her up close rather than just in a magazine – she looks even better in real life!"

"We haven't even got off the plane yet and we've seen a real life supermodel," laughed Poppy. "This trip is going to be amazing. I'm going to have so many cool stories to tell Honey and the other girls at school."

"We're going to see a lot of beautiful people and exciting clothes over the next few days. It's going to be great," said Saffron, squeezing her little cousin's hand and leading her along the aisle. "Come on now. Time to taste the Big Apple!"

Poppy recognized the nickname for New York from her guide book. She smiled, grabbed her lilac backpack and followed Saffron.

Saffron had won
two tickets to New
York Spring Fashion
Week when her shop
was chosen by *Buttons and
Bows* magazine as the Best Clothes
Shop in the area. And because Poppy had
helped her win the prize by being so
helpful to the mystery shopper, who
actually turned out to be Bryony Snow,
the fashion journalist, Saffron decided to
take Poppy on the trip with her.

"I can't wait to see Bryony Snow
again!" said Poppy as they waited for
their bags to come round on the conveyor
belt. "I still can't believe she chose us as
the winners — especially me. After all, I
was only helping out in your shop for
the day!"

"I know, Poppy, but you made a very
good impression on Bryony," replied

Saffron. "It was mainly because of you that my little shop won."

Poppy smiled proudly as they collected their bags and placed them on a trolley. They breezed through passport control and customs and made their way towards the taxi rank. Their New York adventure was really beginning!

"Wow! Bright yellow cabs! I've only ever seen these in movies!" said Poppy.

"Central Park Plaza, please," said Saffron as the driver loaded their bags into the car and the girls climbed into the back seat.

Soon they were whizzing through the dusky streets of New York. Poppy gasped at the height of the buildings and the buzz of people returning home from work along the broad pavements – or sidewalks, as they called them.

After what seemed like no time at all, their taxi pulled over. Poppy looked out of the window to see a magnificent hotel entrance with huge revolving glass doors, lots of plants and shrubs and a vast royal-blue canvas awning. THE CENTRAL PARK PLAZA HOTEL. They'd arrived!

Poppy and Saffron got out of the taxi and thanked and paid the driver; their luggage was immediately whisked off into the lobby. The cousins were due to meet Bryony Snow in the hotel restaurant in half an hour, so they had just enough time to check in, have their luggage taken to their room and freshen up in one of the hotel's amazing powder rooms.

Poppy looked around at all the smart and sophisticated people, as well as lots of gorgeous girls, all dressed up in amazing outfits with fabulous accessories. She thought they were probably in town for Fashion Week just like her and Saffron. Even though there were some quite glamorous ladies in Honeypot Hill, especially at the Beehive Beauty Salon, Poppy had never seen so many fashionable people all in one place before.

They made their way to the grand Park View restaurant, which was on the tenth floor. The dining room was spectacular. It was filled with round tables, all laid with white tablecloths and silver cutlery, as well as flickering candles. There were sweet-smelling white lilies in clear glass vases all around the room, and the huge windows gave them a magnificent view of Central Park. They settled down at their table and ordered a fruit smoothie each. Just as their drinks arrived, Bryony Snow and a striking younger girl burst through the doors.

Bryony was all smiles, shopping bags and apologies.

"I'm so sorry I'm late. There was a sale at Barney's today, and we popped in after the shows and, well, you know how it is . . ."

she explained with a cheeky grin.

Poppy looked at the pretty girl at Bryony's side. Although her face slightly resembled Bryony's, she was very distinctive looking in her own right.

Bryony turned to her. "Oh, I haven't introduced my baby sister, have I? How rude of me! Saffron Sage, Poppy Cotton, please meet Berry!"

Chapter Two

Berry wasn't exactly a baby. She was older than Poppy – probably about the same age as Poppy's cousin Daisy – and looked very cool. She had spirals of long, wild red hair, big brown eyes which looked kind and friendly, and very pale, porcelain skin with a delicate sprinkling of freckles. Poppy thought she looked like she would be great fun.

"Hi, Berry," said Saffron. "How amazing, coming on a trip with your big sister!"

"I know. I'm really lucky," agreed Berry. "Even if Bryony *does* get me to carry all the heavy bags!"

Everyone laughed.

"And is this Princess Poppy here?" asked Berry kindly.

Poppy nodded shyly. She absolutely worshipped older girls and felt very uncool compared to Berry. But Berry smiled so warmly that Poppy knew they were going to be firm friends.

"Let's order some dinner, shall we?" suggested Bryony. "You must be famished after hours of disgusting aeroplane food."

Poppy nodded and looked down at her menu. She didn't want to admit that she absolutely adored the dinky little aeroplane meals, although she *was* definitely hungry.

Once they had ordered from the extensive and somewhat complicated menu, they settled down to getting to know one another properly.

"We've been here for a few days already – lucky it's half term, isn't it?" said Bryony. "I've been going to some of the warm-up shows and doing a few interviews for the magazine – as well as shopping. I'm going to be exhausted by the end of the week at this rate – and bankrupt. Anyway, enough about me! Why don't I let you know what your schedule for the whole trip looks like? Oh, and I should warn you, my little brother, Orlando, is with us too. He's having a swimming lesson just now in the hotel pool."

"I'll tell you a little bit about Orlando so that it's not such a nasty surprise when he does turn up!" said Berry. "Let's see now. He's a little creep with a passion for spiders and worms – *and* putting them in girls' beds. He specializes in wrestling and making Formula One car noises. He hardly ever reads proper books but talks non-stop about super-heroes. He's always just slightly grubby and only eats chicken, cheese or chocolate. He's an expert on the solar system and has been known to dip dog biscuits in chocolate spread as a snack. But otherwise he's adorable and you'll just love him!" she concluded, dripping with sarcasm.

Poppy's face dropped. "Is there *anything* good about Orlando?" she asked.

"He's away doing sport a lot?" offered Berry. "And he always has a spare square of chocolate when you get the munchies. Even if it is stuck to bubble-gum and whatever else he's got at the bottom of his bag!"

Poppy smiled. In a funny way, she couldn't wait to meet Orlando. Surely he couldn't be *that* bad!

Bryony passed Saffron an information sheet about the trip: they had an absolutely packed schedule.

"I don't think I've brought enough pretty clothes with me for all these things," worried Poppy, feeling both nervous and excited about the week ahead.

"Don't worry, sweetheart," said Saffron. "I've brought lots of accessories with me – I'm sure we'll work out excellent outfits for everything."

Itinerary for:

Saffron Sage and
Princess Poppy Cotton:

SPRING FASHION WEEK, NEW YORK

DAY ONE - Fashion shows in Bryant
Park, on 42nd and 6th, city centre
Manhattan – front-row seats for
all shows, including the
Ned Carew Extravaganza,
VIP dining cards and goody bags
provided

DAY TWO - City tour

DAY THREE - Free time and shopping

DAY FOUR - Finale show:
Bridal Extravaganza
by Clara Hughson in the
Carlyle Hotel.

DAY FIVE - Farewell Breakfast
and flight home

"You'll look just great, Poppy," said Berry. "Plus you can borrow some of my stuff if it fits. My sister gets loads of freebies to try to make her write nice things about the designers, and if the clothes are too small for her, she gives them to me!"

"Wow, that's really amazing. You're so lucky!" replied Poppy, wishing that she had a big sister like Bryony.

Bryony had lots of glossy magazines with her, including, of course, several issues of *Buttons and Bows*, and while they waited for their food to arrive, she showed everyone the sorts of designs they would be seeing and which fabulous new designers to watch out for.

"You know what's really 'in' just now?" Bryony told them. "A bit of a sailor theme with a splash of vibrant citrus.

Sounds vile, yeah? But it works sooooo well! In fashion, we're always one whole season ahead, so even though it's springtime just now, here in New York we're looking at the autumn/winter collections. Some of the new themes are just to die for. Especially Ned Carew's stuff. His ideas are at the forefront of haute couture. Shabby-chic meets structured, with a hint of sci-fi – which is, you know, so innovative. And his muse is the most gorgeous of all the supermodels, Tallulah Melage."

"We saw her on our flight!" said Poppy excitedly, suddenly feeling very involved in the conversation. "She looked amazing – even prettier than she does in the magazines!"

Berry's eyes shone. "Wow, I'd love to see Tallulah in the flesh. She makes everything she wears look so good.

But the thing about Ned Carew's designs is that they are so ridiculous – just like fancy dress. You could never wear any of his stuff in real life."

Bryony pulled a face. "But that's the whole point of haute couture, little sister," she said, feeling defensive about Ned Carew – she admired him so much and had achieved a real scoop by securing an interview with him for the next morning. "Anyway, it's my job to follow new trends. Ah – here are our starters. Dig in, everyone."

Chapter Three

Poppy simply adored clothes and fashion
– it was so cool that there was a whole
week devoted to them and that she was
here! As she waited for her main course to
arrive, she flicked though the programme
for Fashion Week. She was very taken
with the pictures she saw – of models,
designers and celebrities. Meanwhile
Saffron, who had studied art and fashion
at college, was absolutely loving all the
fashion chat. She made a mental note of

everything she had seen in Bryony's selection of glossy magazines and resolved to give herself a whole new look while they were in New York. She couldn't wait to try out some of her ideas.

"Watch out, everybody, here comes Orlando!" said Bryony, looking over at the restaurant doorway.

Poppy turned round to see a very scruffy and cheeky-looking boy coming towards them, with wet hair and a sports bag slung over his shoulder. He had red hair like Berry's, with a cute dusting of freckles too.

"I'm starving!" said Orlando, by way of introduction.

"Well, what would you like?" asked Bryony.

"Same as usual?" suggested Orlando, taking a seat.

"And aren't you going to say hello to our guests?" scolded Bryony.

He mumbled "Hi" and then started rummaging in his bag.

 When the delicious main course of warm bread, pasta in tomato sauce, herb-coated corn-fed chicken and rocket salad arrived, Poppy was amazed to see another plate arrive specially for Orlando. A whole pile of chunky chips were served with melted cheese, and on

the side of the plate
was a small dipping
bowl of hot
chocolate sauce.

"That is gross,
monster!" commented
Berry, dying with embarrassment. Her
brother's strange habits hadn't seemed so
bad on the two previous evenings, when
they'd had no guests, but they made her
cringe now.

Poppy and Saffron smiled.

After a scrumptious dessert of raspberry
double-cream ice with shortcake, they all
decided it was time to go to bed. It had
been a long day, especially for Poppy and
Saffron.

They said goodnight and arranged to
meet in the lobby the following morning.
Bryony, Berry and Orlando went to order
a movie to be delivered to their room,

while Poppy and Saffron stepped into a huge elevator and headed for their room on the twenty-fifth floor. They seemed to go up and up for ever and Poppy was quite sure that they were going to burst through the top of the building into the sky. She had never been in such a tall building before.

When Saffron pushed open the door to their room, Poppy could hardly believe her eyes. It smelled wonderful, as if someone had been burning fragrant candles. The carpet was super soft and velvety pink – Poppy couldn't wait to see what it would feel like on her bare feet. The beds were vast and luxurious, with pure white sheets and pretty lavender silk quilts on top. Even though the Hedgerows Hotel in Honeypot Hill was very pretty, it was nothing like this. This was much more spectacular. There were fresh pink roses in

26

glass bowls and the furniture was in the
French style, with ornate gold carvings.
The curtains were a deep violet-purple
with a fleur-de-lis design embossed over
chintz. As for the toiletries in the
bathroom, it was like a perfume
store!

Saffron was itching to explore their surroundings.

"Come and see the view, Poppy!" she exclaimed, stepping onto their enormous balcony, which overlooked Central Park. "This view is amazing. I can't believe that we're in one of the most exciting cities in the whole world. We're going to have a ball."

Poppy smiled in agreement, mesmerized by the size of the city and all the lights as well as by their hectic, exciting schedule for next few days. But soon she was deep in thought, already trying to decide what to wear the next day.

In the morning, Poppy laid all her wash things out in the huge bathroom — she absolutely loved staying in hotels because everything was so luxurious. Lily Ann Peach from the Beehive Beauty Salon had given her lavender bubble bath,

orange-zest body scrub, rose-water moisturizer and safflower lip balm, but Poppy was determined to try out the amazing-looking products supplied by the hotel. She pinned her hair up on top of her head as she set about getting ready for her first day at New York Fashion Week.

After washing and trying out all the
potions, then brushing her hair, Poppy
decided to wear pink pedal-pushers, with
a pretty white cotton top covered in silver
stars. She finished her outfit off with silver
ankle-strap sandals, complete with a
matching shoulder bag. She put her long
blonde hair in bunches, with pink poppy
baubles securing each bunch, sprayed
herself liberally with the gorgeous hotel
perfume, Fleur, then flicked through

the programme again as she waited
for Saffron to get ready.

Saffron was taking absolutely ages in
the bathroom, and what a surprise Poppy
got when she emerged.

"I'm ready! What do you think of my
new look?" asked Saffron, with a twirl.

Poppy was lost for words, which was
most unlike her. Saffron usually dressed
so beautifully and simply in jewel-
coloured cottons and linens with an
ethnic, natural twist, but today she was
dressed like a gothic bride from a scary
movie. She was wearing an ankle-length
black dress, a grey top hat and fingerless
lace gloves. She had applied very heavy
dark eye make-up and plum-coloured
lipstick. Her hair was back-combed
into a high bouffant and sprayed with
so much hairspray even a hurricane
wouldn't move it. The hat sat at a

jaunty angle on top of the candyfloss
hair confection. Poppy thought her
cousin had gone completely mad.

"I've copied one of the looks from one
of Bryony's magazines and the dress is a
sample she lent me. She dropped it
by last night after you'd gone to sleep.
Don't you like it?" asked Saffron.

"Um, it does look very . . . um . . . interesting and . . . um . . . different, Saffron, but you don't look like you any more," said Poppy, being as truthful as she could without hurting Saffron's feelings.

"Oh dear, don't I suit it then? I just wanted a change, with us being in New York and everything. I thought my look was getting a bit, you know, boring, especially after seeing all the glamorous people on the plane and here at the hotel," replied Saffron in a rather subdued voice.

Poppy was worried that her older cousin might cry.

"But Saffron, everyone wants to dress just like you. All my friends think you're the most glamorous and pretty person they've ever met. You always look lovely in your clothes. You don't need to copy people from magazines."

"I suppose you're right, Poppy," sighed Saffron. "I just got a bit swept up in the excitement of it all. Will you help me pick out another outfit?'

"Yes please," Poppy smiled and headed over to Saffron's bulging wardrobe.

While Saffron went to wash out the hairspray and scrub off the make-up, Poppy laid out a turquoise tiered mini-dress with a short pink jacket and gem-studded sandals for her. She was sure her cousin would look her usual gorgeous self.

When Saffron was finally ready, they went down to the lobby to meet the others before heading over to the fashion shows. Poppy was a bit surprised that Orlando was coming along too. She thought he would prefer the hotel sports club. He hadn't really dressed

34

up for the occasion and Poppy couldn't
imagine that he was into fashion at all.
He was wearing army-green combat
shorts, a black rock-band T-shirt and
trainers. He had his bag over his shoulder,
which Poppy thought was bound to be
full of snails, spiders, worms, frogs and
all sorts of foul things. Berry, on the
other hand, looked magnificent. She
was wearing a navy and white striped
mini-dress with footless tights and loads
of funky jewellery, plus a cute red clutch
bag. And Bryony's outfit was pure haute
couture!

"Come on, you lot," she called. "The
taxi's waiting."

Chapter Four

When they arrived at Bryant Park on
42nd and 6th, Poppy was amazed at the
size of the Fashion Week event. There
were several huge air-conditioned tents
set up in a large park. All around, there
were glamorous people wearing huge
sunglasses and amazing hats and outfits,
mainly in black, white or grey. The
models were all taller and thinner
than Poppy expected.

Berry seemed to know the whole

scene inside out. She nudged Poppy.
"Wow, look – there's Tallulah Melage," she
whispered, pointing to one of the models
close by.

"This is so cool!" Poppy whispered in
reply. "Don't you think she's the most
beautiful girl in the whole world?"

"Definitely," agreed Berry, mesmerized
by the model.

Tallulah must have heard their
whispered comments because she turned
to the girls and smiled broadly.

"I'm not pretty first thing in the morning, I promise you, girls. It's all tricks of the trade," she said sweetly, before floating off in a black chiffon mini-dress.

"Wow, she's a really nice person too," said Berry.

"I know," agreed Poppy. "I just can't believe she spoke to us."

"Most models are really rude and unfriendly," said Berry, sounding very knowledgeable. "But I reckon it's just 'cos they're hungry."

"Yeah, probably," agreed Poppy; she wasn't really sure why the models would be hungry, though she did know that she got quite grumpy when she hadn't eaten properly.

Saffron and Bryony came back after registering at Reception and were quite miffed when they found out that they had missed out on a personal chat with

Tallulah Melage. Bryony was secretly
hoping that Tallulah would be there
when she interviewed Ned Carew later
that morning. She was desperate to
meet her.

Bryony handed
out everyone's
official *Buttons and
Bows* name badges, which allowed them
access to all the VIP rooms and the shows.
The girls were absolutely thrilled with
theirs and pinned them on right away.
Orlando was rather less enamoured with
his, and shoved it into his famous bag!

"We have to wear our badges if we
want to wander around the tents and
runways and get into the smart cafés
and everything," explained Berry, taking
Poppy under her wing.

"Um, OK, but what are runways?"
asked Poppy curiously.

"Just the catwalks where the models sashay up and down in their incredible outfits," explained Berry.

"I wish we could go and stare at airport runways instead of this old garbage," moaned Orlando. "Clothes were invented to keep us dry and warm, or cool and comfortable. Everything else is just rubbish. That's what my dad says."

"If you don't like it here, you should have stayed behind at the hotel, moron!" said Berry.

"Enough bickering, you two," said Bryony firmly. "Let me explain what the plan is. First of all, Saffron and I have a couple of 'press only' shows to go to, so you guys can go exploring. Then I've got an interview with Ned Carew. But you can go to any of the other shows so long as you wear your badges, OK?"

Berry and Poppy nodded, while

Orlando swatted a wasp.

"You can roam around freely but you mustn't leave the park, and don't take unofficial routes between the tents — always use the walkways, otherwise you'll get in the way. And if you get lost, go to Reception and we will find you there. Let's meet for lunch over in the VIP restaurant at about one o'clock. Here's a map. Have fun, and remember: *behave* — especially you, Orlando. You're wearing *Buttons and Bows* badges so you're representing the magazine."

"We promise we'll be good," chimed the children.

"Now, Orlando," called Bryony, "if you *are* good, we'll watch a super-hero movie in the hotel later! Come on, Saffron, we should get going."

Berry rolled her eyes. "I *never* get to see any date movies!" she complained.

"That's because you never get asked on any dates," retorted Orlando.

"Yes I do, but I certainly wouldn't tell you about them!" Berry fired back.

"Eeeurgh. Dating makes me feel sick!" said Orlando, pretending to choke and eventually falling to the ground, clutching his throat and throwing his legs straight up in the air.

Poppy laughed. But this was the worst thing to do with Orlando, because it encouraged him to keep doing the 'funny' thing over and over again, until it was no longer funny at all.

Saffron kissed Poppy goodbye and dashed off after Bryony, leaving the three new friends trying to decide what to do and where to go. Orlando started to try on a huge mother-of-the-bride style hat he found lying on a chair until Berry hissed at him to put it down before he got into trouble with its owner.

"I know," she said. "Let's go and collect our Fashion Week goody bags from the sponsor. They've always got amazing stuff in them and it's all free!"

Poppy nodded keenly, while Orlando pretended to skip like a girl and said, "Oooh, yeah, our goody bags!"

Despite the fact that Bryony had warned them about sticking to the main walkways, they couldn't resist taking a short cut between two of the main tents. Orlando led the way confidently and they saw what it was like behind the scenes at Fashion Week, which the girls found absolutely fascinating. There were rails crammed full of outfits being wheeled to and fro, plus shoeboxes and make-up on trolleys. Crates of juice were lying around, as well as spare tent poles and generators used for heating and lighting the tents. People were agitatedly discussing timings, music was playing intermittently and seamstresses dashed about with measuring tapes round their necks and pins in their mouths.

There were models everywhere. Then, as they were walking behind one of the dressing tents, they heard what sounded like someone sobbing so they decided to investigate.

Chapter Five

Poppy, Berry and Orlando peered in
through the flap to see what was going
on. They saw a very frail and rather
familiar-looking girl. She was bent
double, crying buckets.

"I think that's Tallulah!" whispered
Poppy.

They all crouched down to get a
better look and saw that a very short
man, skinny except for his pot belly and
dressed all in black, was talking to her.

"Pull yourself together, Tallulah. I've
only decided that you're not right for this
show. I'm just not feeling your look for
this collection, darling! OK?"

"But you were totally feeling it
yesterday when we had the final fittings
and dress rehearsal," sobbed Tallulah.

"It *is* Tallulah. And that's Ned Carew,"
whispered Berry as the children strained
to hear. "I bet Bryony wouldn't admire

him so much if she could hear him talking now!"

Poppy nodded.

"Well, I'm not feeling your look now, sweetheart," Ned continued, seeming totally oblivious to how upset Tallulah was. "I've got a younger girl lined up – fresh from Europe. She's so much more now. I just want what's best for the collection and so should you. And right now, that's not you! That's all I'm saying. Don't take things so personally, yeah? Get over it."

Poppy was shocked. She couldn't imagine anyone in the world being more beautiful or perfect than Tallulah, and she was really young too. Poppy thought she was probably about the same age as Saffron, although she'd been a world-famous model since she was Daisy's age.

Ned strolled off as if he didn't have a care in the world, leaving poor Tallulah in a crumpled heap.

"I'm over. He hates me," she said to herself. "What am I going to do?"

Berry went in through the gap in the tent, followed by Poppy and Orlando. She walked up to the model and handed her a tissue.

"We still think you look lovely!" she said shyly.

Tallulah managed a small smile and sniffed. "Thank you! It's just so awful that I've been dropped by Ned – he's like God around here. No one else is

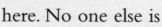

going to want to work with me now."

"But he's really wicked. Just forget him," suggested Berry.

"I'd like to but I don't know what else to do. Modelling is all I know – I've been doing it since I was quite young," explained Tallulah.

"Don't worry, Tallulah," said Berry. "You're better than he is – I'm sure you'll work something out."

"You're such sweet kids. Listen, I'd better go and call my agent. But thanks for being so nice," said Tallulah, trying to compose herself. "I think you're probably the only honest and genuine people around here."

And with that she pulled a phone out of her bag and went off to make her call.

"That Ned guy is a right shark and deserves a taste of his own medicine. I've got an idea," said Orlando as soon as

Tallulah was out of earshot. "Quick, let's follow him . . ."

Poppy looked at Berry, who shrugged her shoulders and said, "Why not? He's been horrid to poor Tallulah. I don't care how famous or talented he is, he shouldn't be allowed to get away with treating people like that."

Outside the tent, Ned Carew was untying his beloved little pooch, Chi-Chi.

"Come on, Chi-Chi-kins, Daddy needs brunch," he said, heading off in the direction of the restaurant tent.

The two girls followed Orlando, who

followed Ned Carew through a maze
of tents all the way to the VIP hospitality
tent. At one point they lost him, but he
had just stopped to give an autograph
to an adoring fan.

"You're just the king, Ned. We love
your styles," she told him.

He smiled and said casually, "It's what
I do, honey."

Finally Ned Carew tied Chi-Chi to
another pole and went into the lavish
VIP tent.

"I'll have the full English all-day

breakfast, and sharpish," he demanded. "Extra mushrooms, eggs sunny side up, pancakes and hash browns – and hey, do me a side order of French fries. And I like organic maple syrup. Get me a full milk mocha latte too, with sprinkles."

Poppy noticed that he didn't say please or thank you, which she thought was very rude.

"Gross. He's so greedy!" said Berry.

But Orlando wasn't listening. Instead he was fumbling around in his bag.

"Ah-ha! Just what I was looking for," he said, pulling some things out. "We need to distract him for a moment when his food arrives. I've got some salt and vinegar sachets for his coffee, and hot chilli powder and extra-strong mustard powder for his fry-up, all courtesy of the Central Park Plaza Hotel. We can watch him from here and see his face screw up

when he tastes his brunch with my special
seasoning."

Poppy was starting to realize that she
and Orlando had quite a lot in common.
She liked the way he thought. "Cool idea,
Orlando. He deserves it," she giggled.

When Ned's vast platter of food
arrived, Poppy was tasked with creating a
diversion to make him look away from
the table, giving Orlando the chance to
put his plan into action.

"What shall I do?" she asked as they
saw Ned licking his lips in eager
anticipation.

"Just think of something. Quickly,"
instructed Orlando.

The only thing Ned seemed to care

about was his little dog, Chi-Chi, so
Poppy decided to untie the fluffy white
pooch and carry her in to Ned as if she
had just found her roaming about looking
for her master.

"Excellent plan, princess!" said
Orlando. "Off you go."

Poppy stroked the sweet little dog and
undid her leash, then popped her into her
large shoulder bag and carried her
undetected through the entrance of the
hospitality tent. No one stopped her,
probably because they thought she was
the daughter of a designer, and she made
her way over to where Ned was sitting.

Chapter Six

Chi-Chi yapped frantically when she
saw Ned, and he jumped up as soon as
he saw her peeking out of Poppy's bag.

"What you doin' with my dog, kid?"
he barked at Poppy.

"Sorry, sir – she was lost and someone
said she belonged to you," said Poppy,
desperately trying not to laugh when
she caught sight of Berry and Orlando
pulling faces and giving her the
thumbs-up.

Ned took Chi-Chi in his arms and kissed and hugged her.

"I'm sorry, sir, we don't allow pets inside the VIP tent," said a waitress as she arrived at his table.

"OK, lady," said Ned irritably. "I'm just going to take her out and this time I'll tie her up more securely, won't I, Chi-Chi, darling?"

As Ned made his way out to deal with the dog, Orlando moved in stealthily and smothered the fry-up with mustard powder and hot chilli pepper, and doused the pale mocha latte with lashings of salt and vinegar. When he was finished, he took up his position outside the tent with Berry again. By the time Poppy ran round to join them, Ned was sitting down once more, greedily eyeing his enormous brunch.

As soon as he took a mouthful of food,

his face began to
crease up and his
lips pursed together
in an expression of
disgust. He looked as if
he was going to explode.
He spat the mouthful of food back out
onto his plate and quickly took a gulp of
coffee to put out the fire on his tongue,
only to choke and splutter, and eventually
spit that out too. Then he began to sneeze
and cough, gasping for breath, his face
growing redder and redder as he undid

his collar and flapped
his hand in front
of his mouth like
a fan. Berry,
Orlando and
Poppy could
hardly contain
their giggles.

"Someone is trying to murder me before my big show! Help! Call the police. Call nine one one. I'm dying!" Ned spluttered as the other diners looked on in horror.

A whole bevy of waitresses swarmed around him, but no one was able to calm him down. He was calling for water, ice and a full investigation into who had poisoned him.

"Job well done!" said Orlando, patting his trusty bag.

"Let's get out of here quickly," said Berry sensibly. "Why don't we go and check out some shows now? Oh, and we never did pick up those goody bags, did we? Shall we do it now?"

"Yes please," said Poppy. "I can't wait to see what's in them – and to see a real fashion show."

"OK," said Orlando, "but I'm not finished with him yet!"

Berry rolled her eyes. "He won't stop until he's caught," she said to Poppy. "He doesn't believe in quitting while he's ahead!"

The goody bag was much bigger than Poppy had expected, and full of so many lovely things. There was a classic white T-shirt, funky jewellery, a brand-new type of perfume called Liberty, as well as a beautiful leather-bound design pad, pens and pencils. The bag was tied up with ribbon and had a fresh pale-pink rose attached to it.

"Hey, a show's about to start in that

tent over there," said Berry, looking at a notice board. "It's Nick Lamont. His stuff is pretty weird but he puts on really great shows. It's like being in a costume drama! Let's go and check it out."

Poppy and her two new friends sat perfectly still as they took in the runway show from their front-row seats. Poppy was amazed to find that the theme of the show was "Aliens". She didn't think anyone in real life could ever wear any of the outfits; the models were quite scary-looking and had crazy hair and make-up.

"What do you think?" whispered Berry.

"Um, I think it's a bit strange," said Poppy, hoping her friend thought the same.

"Exactly what I was thinking," agreed Berry. "I mean, no one is actually going

to wear this stuff."

Orlando was fast asleep but fortunately not snoring! Once the show was over, they woke him up and decided to flop on the grassy square in the main courtyard until it was time to meet Bryony and Saffron.

"I know!" said Poppy. "Let's sketch our own designs. They've got to be better than the ones in Aliens!"

"Good idea," said Berry, opening her goody bag to get out her sketchpad.

"Saffron has taught me to do proper fashion drawings like the ones she does," said Poppy. "I just adore drawing clothes."

"Me too," said Berry. "I'd love to be a fashion designer just like Saffron one day. Not like the silly pretentious designers here."

Much as Orlando tried to distract them, the girls were very focused on their drawing. So much so that he eventually gave up with the tormenting and went off to explore.

"What kind of stuff are you going to design?" Poppy asked.

"I dunno – how about you?" said Berry.

"Well, I really love New York, or what

I've seen of it so far," replied Poppy. "Maybe we should do designs based on this city?"

"Hey, nice idea. I'm going to do a Big Apple dress!" said Berry. "But it will be something we could really wear, something pretty."

"And I'll do one based on the dress the Statue of Liberty wears. It'll be a perfect party dress," decided Poppy.

After sketching for a while, Berry looked up and was amazed to see one of her fashion heroines walking by.

"Poppy, look!" she whispered. "That's Clara Hughson over there. She's my absolute favourite designer of all time. She makes the most amazing party and wedding dresses. They look like they're out of fairytales."

"Wow!" said Poppy. "That's so cool."

"I sent her some of my designs once

too," explained Berry breathlessly, "and she replied and said she really liked my ideas. Oh my gosh, she's coming this way – look!"

"Hey, girls," said Clara. "You look about the same ages as my daughters back home. Which of these tops do you think they'd prefer?"

She held up two different styles, and Poppy and Berry both pointed to the same striped top.

"Just what I thought!" agreed Clara, glancing at their pads. "What are you guys sketching?"

"We're just trying to design some things that people can really wear, not like the stuff we've seen in the shows," explained Berry.

"I know exactly what you mean, girls," replied Clara. "Shock tactics are so tedious — I've always tried to design for real women. These look really great, you know. They're so fresh. Tell you what, girls, I've got a spare slot at the end of my Bridal Extravaganza at the Carlyle Hotel in three days' time. If you can come up with a few more cute ideas like these, I'll give you the slot! Oh — I'm Clara Hughson, by the way. The only snag is that you'll have to make up the outfits yourselves and model them too. It would be like putting on a whole little show of your own. Are you interested?"

"Wow! That sounds amazing," exclaimed Berry. "We'd love to do it, wouldn't we, Poppy?"

Poppy nodded enthusiastically, not fully understanding what was involved, but thinking it sounded cool anyway.

"Call me and let me know if it's coming together," said Clara as she handed them her business card. Then she looked at Berry. "You know what, I feel like I've seen your work before."

Berry smiled and explained about the fan letter and designs.

"What a coincidence!" exclaimed Clara. "We were destined to meet, obviously. You've really got talent, Berry, and so has your friend."

And with that, she was off to mingle with the throngs of journalists, designers and models who were wafting around the glamorous event.

"Now I really am dreaming. I've met my *absolute* all-time favourite designer and a world-famous supermodel on the same day, and we're going to put on our own show. This is amazing!" said Berry.

"I know!" Poppy could hardly believe how exciting this trip was turning out to be. It was just like something out of a storybook!

Just then Orlando came back from his recce looking worryingly happy.

Berry was sure he was up to some sort of mischief.

"Gosh, it's time for lunch with Bryony and Saffron already!" she said. "We'd better go to the food tent now or we'll be late."

Chapter Seven

"Hi, girls and boy!" Saffron smiled as
Poppy, Berry and Orlando sat down.
"How's your morning been?"

"Totally cool!" said Berry.

"We've had the best time ever," agreed
Poppy. "Just wait until you hear about it
all. I love Fashion Week!"

Berry took up the story and told
Saffron and Bryony all about the shows,
the goody bags, their sketches and about
Clara Hughson's amazing offer (she

decided that it might be best to leave the Ned Carew episode out for now).

"How amazing!" enthused Saffron. "We've had a positively dull time compared to you. I'd love to help you with the Clara Hughson show, but it's going to be hard work – there's hardly any time."

"Yeah," agreed Bryony, "you've been having a much better time than us. My big interview with Ned Carew was cancelled at the last moment for some reason his publicist didn't make clear. But never mind about that. What a mad dream, Clara Hughson offering you guys a slot. I'm going to take you two lucky charms everywhere with me."

Berry looked up and was surprised to see Tallulah at the entrance of the tent, looking a bit lost and lonely. She waved, and Tallulah started heading towards them.

Saffron and Bryony could hardly believe
their eyes.

"Do you mind if we say how we met
you, Tallulah?" asked Berry when the
supermodel arrived at their table. She
pulled up a chair for her.

"No, go ahead. It's going to be quite
obvious during this afternoon's show

anyway," responded the broken-hearted model wearily.

Saffron and Bryony were shocked when they heard the full story of Ned Carew's decision to drop his top muse so abruptly and insensitively.

"He's mad! Quite mad!" said Bryony. "I only ever buy Ned Carew because I want to look as stylish as you! I don't feel nearly as enthusiastic about his Extravaganza this afternoon now, but I've got to go as part of my brief from the magazine, especially since he cancelled the interview this morning."

"Seemingly he has a younger model who's in the show instead of me. He only discovered her recently, in Europe. I guess I'm history now. If only he'd told me before I flew out here. I feel very hurt and humiliated," said Tallulah. "But as for your interview, I've heard he's not

feeling too well," she said, winking at the children. "Indigestion or something."

The three children looked pointedly at their menus, all blushing furiously.

"Poor you," said Saffron. "No one deserves to be treated like that. Why don't you stay and have lunch with us? Maybe that will cheer you up."

"Oh, that would be lovely, thanks," smiled Tallulah.

They ordered a wonderful-sounding lunch of asparagus and parmesan risotto followed by blueberry pavlova, all washed down with sparkling organic apple juice.

"Perhaps I could do a really big spread on you in *Buttons and Bows*, to keep your name in the fashion arena," suggested Bryony over lunch. "It would make up for me not getting the interview with Ned Carew and also show him that you don't need him to succeed."

"How kind. That sounds good. We could hook up again back home, after Fashion Week," suggested Tallulah.

Soon the conversation turned back to the Clara Hughson slot, which was all news to Tallulah.

"This will be a show like no other!" stated Berry. "We can showcase Saffron's designs *and* our ideas too!"

"Yeah!" agreed Poppy. "Clara really liked our designs."

"It's all going to be incredibly tight, time-wise," said Bryony. "Let's see – we've only got a couple of days to pull it off."

"Well, if I can help in any way, I'd be very happy to do so," said Tallulah. "I can sew pretty well after all these years of watching seamstresses."

"Thanks — that would be awesome. Do you think you could also model in the show too?" asked Berry shyly.

"Of course I could, if that's any use," said Tallulah modestly.

Throughout lunch all the girls chatted excitedly about ideas for the mini-show they were to produce. Meanwhile, under the pretext of needing the loo, Orlando excused himself from the table;

when he came back, he looked very
pleased with himself indeed. Poppy and
Berry knew he was up to something —
they just didn't know what . . .

Chapter Eight

After lunch they waved goodbye to
Tallulah, promising to call her later, and
reluctantly headed off to Ned Carew's
show. Much to the girls' surprise, Orlando
seemed to know the route rather well.

Poppy and Berry sat next to Saffron
and Bryony in the front row even though
none of them were very excited about the
show now that they knew what a
dreadful man Ned was. As the girls
chatted, no one noticed Orlando sneaking

off to check on his latest bit of mischief –
an invisible trip-wire across the runway.

Just then, the lights dimmed and Ned
Carew made his entrance. His eyes were
watery and his face was bright red – he
was probably still burning up from all
the hot chilli pepper and mustard on his
brunch! He waved to the cheering crowd
and made his way to the podium to
introduce the show. But as he neared the
stand, as if in slow motion, he tripped,
arms and legs flailing. He fell flat on his
face. *Splat!* It also became clear that he
was wearing a wig. His hair was tilted
to one side, revealing an expanse
of polished head which
wasn't nearly as
tanned as
his face.

There was a moment of silence, followed by nervous giggling from the crowd. Ned dragged himself up and glared at the audience. He tried to regain his composure, and some minders dashed over to help him to the microphone. He began to talk, but sadly for him, someone had snipped the wires.

Orlando grinned with complete satisfaction as Ned Carew swept furiously from the stage.

"Heads will roll for this!" the designer screeched. "No one makes a fool of Ned Carew!"

Everyone was starting to shift around uncomfortably in their seats when, all of a sudden, Ned's new model, Amélie, appeared on stage. She seemed rather confused and embarrassed, as if she had been pushed on from the wings. Someone must have decided that the show must go

on, but she was far
from happy about it.
There was no music
and the audience
were all chatting
and laughing. She
tried to sashay down
the runway in a very
tight-fitting sailor suit
and platform shoes,
with what looked like an enormous chef's
hat on her head. The audience clearly
thought the whole thing was rather
ridiculous now that all the cool trappings
of the fashion show had fizzled away.
Before long there were even some boos.
Amélie's face began to crumple. Her
debut was proving to be a disaster and
she was furious. She turned and sped back
up the catwalk so fast that she nearly
tripped in her high heels.

"I quit from Ned Carew!" she cried, fleeing from the stage. "He's a loser!"

Poppy and Berry couldn't wait to tell Tallulah all about the Extravaganza. They knew that Orlando had played a huge part in giving Ned Carew his comeuppance and they were secretly very proud of him.

Chapter Nine

The next morning, Poppy and Saffron
woke early. They were very excited about
their planned tour of New York, which
Tallulah was going to come on too. They
met her, Bryony, Orlando and Berry for
an early breakfast at the hotel, and as
they ate, they told Tallulah all about
Ned's disastrous show.

"Wow! I almost wish I'd gone now,"
she said. "I bet his face was a picture! I
wonder who sabotaged his show – he's

made so many enemies over the years, it could be anyone."

"Probably someone who thinks Ned's just a total idiot who deserves a taste of his own medicine," said Orlando with a smile as he tucked into chocolate cereal with chocolate milk.

"We'll have to get back here by tea time so we can start work on our show for Clara," said Bryony, starting to fret about how little time they had to put their show together and wondering whether it was even possible.

"Well, we'd better get going then," said Saffron. "I can't wait to see some more of this amazing city!"

After a scrumptious breakfast of pancakes, maple syrup and scrambled eggs, the whole gang made their way to the pick-up point for their city tour. Poppy had a camera with her and took lots of photos of all the places she'd read about in her guide book – Wall Street with its banks, Broadway, where all the theatres were, and, of course, the magnificent Empire State Building. Poppy absolutely adored the carriage ride around

Central Park — it made her feel just like a
princess. But her favourite bit of the
whole tour was a special surprise
organized by Tallulah.

"You've all been so sweet, I wanted
to do something nice for you," she
explained, "so I asked my publicist
to arrange for Macy's, the best
department store in town, to close down
for an hour so we can have private
shopping time."

Poppy and Berry thought they would
burst with excitement.

"Wow!" exclaimed Bryony. "Thanks,
that's amazing! I've always wanted
Macy's all to myself!"

When the party arrived at the world-
famous store, they were treated like
royalty. Poppy hardly knew where to start
as she took in the perfumes, make-up and
jewellery, clothes, shoes and accessories.

"Follow me," said Tallulah, "I know this shop better than my own apartment!"

Poppy had the time of her life. She bought the twins a toy each with her dollars, which she kept in her sequinned purse. For Archie she chose a bright-green engine; for Angel, a teddy in a ballet tutu with a bow on her head. She bought some fancy perfume for Mum and a beautiful cashmere scarf for Dad. Then they all got together in the haberdashery department and picked up sewing things, some fabulous fabric and masses of gorgeous accessories for their show.

Their trip to Macy's seemed to fly by, and soon they were back with the tour guide. The next stop was the quay where they were to catch a ferry for a trip out to the Statue of Liberty.

As they approached the statue, Poppy was transfixed.

"Isn't she magnificent?" said Berry.

"Yeah," replied Poppy, "and she looks so strong and brave. I'm definitely going to make a Liberty dress for our show."

Poppy loved the tour of Liberty Island, where she saw the statue's original torch up close, and as she looked back over New York's spectacular harbour, she felt as though she was the luckiest girl in the world.

Chapter Ten

After a full day of sightseeing they
stopped for a smoothie and a muffin
and then returned to the hotel for a team
meeting. It was time to get to work on
their show. The first job was to call
Clara to check that everything was
still OK for their slot. Once Bryony
had the official thumbs-up, she
started to make a list of what had to
be done.

"What is the main idea behind these

designs going to be?" asked Saffron
sensibly.

"We want to theme it around New
York – that was Poppy's idea," explained
Berry.

"Great idea, Poppy," said Saffron. "I
love it! But what aspect of the city are
you going to emphasize?"

Poppy thought for a moment.
"Freedom. The freedom there is here to
be what you want to be and dress how
you want to dress."

"What a brilliant idea, girls," said
Tallulah. "It's so refreshing. We're all
puppets for the big designers – I only
realized it yesterday when Ned dropped
me from his show. I think we should
show wearable designs which real
people might actually wear for every
day things."

Everyone agreed that they were onto

something here. Their show had to be
different from the big shows in order to
stand out, and after their experience of
the obsessive control of Ned Carew, and
some of the ludicrous outfits they had
seen during the week – including Saffron's
short-lived new look – they all wanted
to do a show for real people. So, with the
concept firmly in place, they set about
designing, cutting, pinning, stitching and
assembling the outfits.

Saffron showed them
all the fashion goodies
she had brought from
Honeypot Hill. There
was an adorable knitted
daisy-shape hat made by
Poppy's mum, plus other
cute hats and head-dresses;
there were several pieces of
exquisite jewellery made by
Holly Mallow; there were
pretty coloured silk scarves
made by Saffron herself,
and a wonderful crocheted
poncho made for Poppy by
Granny Bumble (Poppy's
best friend, Honey, had one
too). As everyone wanted
an early night, with such a
big preparation day ahead
of them, they ordered room

service, then snuggled down for the night.

The next morning they all met back in Bryony's room and got to work straight away. As Berry, Poppy and Saffron sketched, Bryony and Tallulah cut and sewed. After about an hour there was a knock at the door. Orlando, who was at a bit of a loose end but was trying to be helpful, offered to play butler and went to see who was there.

"Hi, I'm Delia," said the pleasant-faced lady standing in the corridor. "I work for Clara Hughson as a seamstress. She thought you might need some help with your show, so here I am."

"Come in, come in," said Bryony as she rushed over to the door. "How wonderful to see you, and how kind of Clara to spare you. Oh, and you've got a sewing machine too!"

Orlando helped Delia carry everything into the room and she set about helping the girls immediately.

The rest of the day passed in a haze of fittings, cuttings, sewing and laughing. There was hardly any time to get excited or admire their creations but Poppy was sure everything was going to look splendid in time for the show. As they worked, they planned the running order. It was decided that Saffron, Bryony, Orlando and Delia would help backstage, while Poppy and Berry would do the modelling – along with Tallulah, of course.

"Tallulah?" said Berry as they sat

sewing buttons onto the dresses. "Any chance you can show Poppy and me how we should walk on the runway?"

Poppy looked up from her sketchbook. This sounded like fun. Bryony put on some pop music and they all followed Tallulah around the room, trying to walk like supermodels, with books balanced on their heads. As far as Orlando was concerned, things were getting just too

silly, so he headed off to the hotel pool.

"I don't think I've been this excited about a show since my first ever one," laughed Tallulah. "I'm so glad that things have worked out like this."

"As long as there are no trip-wires, I think I'll be just fine!" giggled Poppy.

"Let's empty that bag of Orlando's," said Berry, laughing.

By the evening, everyone was feeling tired but confident that they had a lovely collection to showcase the next day. They decided to go out to an ice-cream parlour to celebrate and treat themselves to some delicious sundaes.

Chapter Eleven

Midway through the next morning, with
the show only hours away, they packed
all their wonderful creations, including
the accessories, into tissue-lined boxes and
called down to the lobby to order three
taxis to take them over to the Carlyle
Hotel, where their show was due to start
later that day.

When everything was ready, in an
effort to forget their nerves, Poppy and
Berry decided to take a peek at Clara's

bridal show from the wings. It was a
heavenly display of romantic white and
candyfloss-coloured gowns. There were
metres of tulle, silk organza and taffeta,
plus duchesse satin galore and the most
gorgeous flowers. Even though the dresses
were stunning, Poppy still thought that
none of them were quite as wonderful as
Saffron's wedding dress had been.

Clara Hughson came on stage at the
end of her show to a standing ovation. She
thanked all her models, assistants and
seamstresses, and then she thanked

everyone for coming and encouraged
them to stay for the extra part to the show.

"I think you are in for a lovely surprise.
Some young designers have really caught
my eye and they are about to delight you
with a display of their own designs. The
show, ladies and gentleman, is called
'Freedom'. I think it speaks for itself."

The audience clapped and cheered and
the photographers got into position. The
main lights dimmed and the spotlights
shone. Then some very fast pop music
started up.

Poppy was first on, opening the show in a cute ivory-white shift dress, embroidered with autumn leaves, teamed up with flat mid-calf-length boots and her mum's daisy hat. She had an absolute ball posing at the end of the runway and had to be reminded to make her way off stage so that Berry could come on! She tried to remember everything Tallulah had shown her about how to walk on a runway, but as soon as she was out there she forgot all the tips and just walked naturally. This seemed to delight the crowd and the photographers, who were all cheering her on.

Snap! Snap! went the cameras again as Berry came on in her amazing bright-green Big Apple dress. It had a simple boat neckline and a tulip skirt. Berry wore it with black leggings and flat pumps. The crowd roared with approval

and Berry got totally into the walk and
the posing, complete with hands on hips
and a flick of her fabulous red hair, which
looked incredible with the vibrantly
coloured dress.

Poppy and Berry made their changes
quickly, with help from Saffron, Bryony,
Delia and even Clara herself, and each
time they came on in
their simple but
stunning designs, they
received a rapturous
reception from the
crowd and the
photographers kept
on clicking. The
audience gasped
with surprise and
delight when Tallulah
made her entrance
and sashayed down

the runway in a pretty appliquéd skirt
and peasant blouse combo, accessorized
with Holly Mallow's
fabulous jewellery.

   For the finale,
Poppy appeared in
her Liberty dress –
inspired by her
trip to the Statue
of Liberty. She
stepped elegantly
down the runway
with her arm
outstretched, holding
a bouquet of flowers in place of a
torch, which she then presented to
Tallulah. The photographers clicked non-
stop and Poppy smiled and posed so
much that her mouth went numb.

   The audience loved the show and
stamped their feet and clapped their

hands – the designs were such a refreshing
change. Clara Hughson was thrilled with
the result. She came out onto the stage
and waited while more cheering went on,
then presented Saffron and Bryony with
bouquets of wild flowers.

"Firstly, I'd like to let you know that I
will be stocking the Freedom range in all
my stores next season. Secondly, and most
importantly, all my thanks for this real
treat today go to Saffron Sage, British
designer from Honeypot Hill, Bryony

Snow, fashion writer from *Buttons and Bows*, Berry Coleman, fashionista, Tallulah Melage, supermodel, and Poppy Cotton, fashion princess!"

Everyone on stage bowed and curtsied, including Orlando, who had played his own unique part in Fashion Week. Poppy twirled and danced to the music, which had started up again.

After the show Poppy and the girls had to pose for lots more photos. And then there were interviews with all the top papers and TV channels. Poppy had never felt so important. She couldn't wait to tell her family and friends back in Honeypot Hill about her amazing adventure in New York.

As they all said goodbye to Clara, she produced an envelope for them.

"Thank you so much for giving me back my faith in real fashion. Here are some tickets to *Cinderella*, performed by the New York City Ballet. It starts in two hours – I hope you can make it!"

Bryony thanked Clara for the tickets: everyone was thrilled. Saffron thanked her for giving them such a wonderful opportunity, and they said their final goodbyes.

They loaded all their stuff into some waiting cabs and headed back towards their hotel. Poppy couldn't wait for the ballet show. It was their final New York

treat, and she knew just what she was
going to wear – the Liberty dress!

THE END

Turn over to read an extract from
the next Princess Poppy book,
The Rescue Princess . . .

Chapter One

Poppy loved cosy nights in, especially Fridays. School was over for another week, and when the weather was cold, there was always a roaring fire in the sitting room at Honeysuckle Cottage, which made things seem even cosier. The smell of Mum's home-baked bread and Victoria sponges, both regular weekend treats, wafted in from the kitchen stove. But tonight Poppy was even happier than usual because she was having her first ever sleepover. Honey, Mimosa, Sweetpea and Abigail had come over straight after school and were all staying the night. They had been planning and looking forward to the sleepover for weeks.

"My cousin Daisy and her friends have sleepovers all the time, although she has hers in the summer house, not in her bedroom," explained Poppy as she laid out everybody's sleeping bags neatly on the cushions Mum had put out for the girls to sleep on.

"Don't Daisy and her friends do lots of beauty treatments when they have sleepovers?" piped up Honey, who was quite a fan of Poppy's older cousin. "I wish we could do that."

"Well, actually, we can. Come and see," said Poppy excitedly. "I went to see Lily Ann Peach today at the Beehive Beauty Salon and she's given me all this

stuff. Look!"

"Wow! Make-up!" said Sweetpea. "My mum never lets me wear make-up. This is so cool. I love that bright red lipstick!"

"And sparkly eye shadow," gasped Abigail.

"Look at all the creams and lotions too!" said Honey as she examined the pretty bottles and jars. "Yippee!"

"I told you I'd sort it out, didn't I?" laughed Poppy.

"Ugh, what's that?" wondered Mimosa, pointing at a glass jar of what looked like guacamole. "Do we eat it with dipping chips?"

"No, silly," said Poppy knowledgably. "It's avocado face pack. Lily Ann said to spread it on our faces then wash it off after about half an hour."

"Cool . . . but what's it for?" asked Abigail.

"Um . . . it makes your face glow or something," muttered Poppy, who wasn't quite sure of the point of it herself but knew it seemed incredibly grown-up, if a little disgusting and slimy.

"Right," she continued, "I've made a plan for tonight. We can't waste a single nanosecond because this doesn't happen very often. Have you all brought the things we agreed on?"

Everybody nodded.

"OK then. Let's run through the list of what everyone should have with them," said Poppy, clutching her very efficient-looking clipboard.

Nightie, slippers + dressing gown
Wash bag
Clean clothes for tomorrow
Books
Camera
Leotards, dance shoes,
fairy wings and tiaras.

All the friends rummaged about in
their backpacks.

"Yes," they chorused. "Got everything."

"Good. So here's the plan. Let's start
with the posters for cousin Daisy's band,
the Beach Babes. Have you brought your
art set, Honey?"

Honey produced a fabulous box of art
materials which her mum and dad had
given her on their last visit to Honeypot
Hill, complete with several big sheets of

white paper, some stencils, stickers and a calligraphy set.

"Check," she said.

"Good, that's the posters sorted then," continued Poppy. "After that we can start the beauty treatments. I've got all that stuff which we've just seen. Very well done, Poppy Cotton, good job," she said, patting herself on the back.

All the girls laughed. Poppy was great fun, even if she *did* have a bit of a bossy streak.

"After that, we need to practise our dance routine for the Beach Babes' next gig. Mimosa, did you bring your big sister's cool CDs?"

"Yep, here they are," replied Mimosa, and held up the bright pink CD player and karaoke machine she had brought with her as well.

"Excellent. After that it will be supper time. Yum-yum! Mum's cooked something 'sensible'. Have you got the goodies, Sweetpea?"

"Yes, I most certainly do!" said Sweetpea proudly, showing off a large bag of mixed sweets from the General Store. The girls were hardly ever allowed to eat sweets.

"Wow!" said Abigail. "I hope my dad doesn't find out!"

"And after supper, when Mum's tucked

us up in bed, it's officially 'Scary Story Time'. I've been to the library and got these!" announced Poppy.

The girls drew closer to examine the books Poppy was holding out: *Ghostly Galleons: Pirate and Mermaid Spirits*, plus *Highwaymen and Other Robbers*. And the worst ever was *Witches' Way*.

"Oooh, they all sound horrible," shuddered Honey.